Tiana and Briana

The Problem with Ms. Perfect

Written by Doreen Allen

&

Illustrated by Jinelys Cosme Torres

This is a work of fiction. All of the characters, organizations, and events portrayed in this novel are either products of the author's imagination or are used fictitiously.

ISBN-13: 978-1533062604
ISBN-10: 1533062609
First Edition: August 2015

Editing/Formatting: Inspite of Enterprises LLC
Cover/Illustrations: Jinelys Cosme Torres
Photography: John Lewis Studios

DEDICATION

This book is dedicated to my daughter, Tiana, who reminded me that I deserved the best. To Brooke and Brandon, thank you for being the best and for bringing out the best in me.

ACKNOWLEDGEMENTS

God is amazing! He has loved me and guided me through the entire process of this book and He deserves all the glory and praise.

I want to thank my beautiful butterfly angel, my first born, Tiana, for the time we shared together. Although it was God's will for you to return home, you left behind memories that can never be erased. Your mannerism, sassiness, and wit were the inspiration for this book. You will never be forgotten and now others will love the girl whom I loved so much.

Thank you to my lovely and ambitious daughter, Brooke. You are not simply a daughter to me, but a friend as well. I appreciate your support and loyalty. I know you will be an even bigger success than you are now because you won't settle for anything less.

Thank you to my last born and only son Brandon. You are an even bigger joy now than the day you were born. Thank you for being my strength, my protector, my sunshine, and my fresh air. Take your time son. Whatever you aspire to be, will be great.

Much love to my 2014 - 2015 fifth and sixth grade students. You all were encouraging, entertaining and without you, I don't know how I would've survived my biological children growing up so quickly and not needing me as much. You became my babies and I love each and every one of you.

Many thanks to Pamela Harris Williams for answering all my questions and helping to make my dream of writing a book a reality.

Much gratitude to Jinelys Cosme Torres for bringing my girls to life and capturing their beauty.

Thank you to my Facebook friends who helped to make this possible and cheered me on as the process unfolded.

TABLE OF CONTENTS

CHAPTER 1

Waking from the long drive, Tiana and Briana looked out the window to absorb the sights of their new neighborhood. The family was relocating because their father, Marvin Taylor, received a promotion and it required them to move. Mr. Taylor was an architect and he designed big buildings and was now in charge of the new office in Pine Valley, Pennsylvania. Tiana really felt some kind of way about the move. She turned to Paprika, the family dog, who she believed loved her more than her twin sister Briana. Paprika always knew how she felt and ironically he seemed to always feel the same way.

Not caring who heard, Tiana said nicely and loudly, "They just uprooted me in the middle of the night. I didn't even get to say goodbye to all of my friends. I'm really gonna hate it here."

Paprika, as if agreeing, placed his paw on Tiana's shoulder. Mrs. Taylor turned and gave Tiana a look that reminded her that she'd better get it together or else. With a loud huff, she turned back to look out the window. Briana, on the other hand, was extremely excited about the move and believed Paprika was feeling the same since he loved her more than Tiana and he always felt the same way she did.

She turned to him and whispered, "I'm so glad I got to say goodbye to everyone, even my favorite teacher Mrs. Nathan." Paprika, as if agreeing, licked her face.

"I even had time to get everyone's email addresses so that I can keep in touch. I'm really gonna like it here."

She turned to face the window again and pressed her nose even harder into the glass. Both girls rode in silence the rest of the way and Paprika, wanting to be loved by both girls, didn't know what to do. After a while, the car came to a slow roll and Tiana and Briana couldn't believe what they saw.

As their mom drove down Sycamore Street, the street that their new home was on, they saw a playground and lots of kids playing. Briana became really excited and her long ponytails, full of curls, bounced up and down with her every move. Tiana had a little glimmer in her eye, but she dare not let on that she too was somewhat curious. Feeling the vibe from the girls, Paprika barked with excitement.

"That's a really nice playground girls, isn't it?" Mrs. Taylor said looking at the girls in the rearview mirror.

"Oh yes it is!" said Briana.

"It's okay," said Tiana. "I've seen better."

"I would think a playground like that could help with the transition of the move from your old school and friends. I'm sure you could have many of days of playing on the swings with the other kids." Mrs. Taylor continued, aware that Tiana was more excited than she let on.

"I guess," Tiana whispered with a little more enthusiasm.

"I'm sure of it mom," said Briana.

"I didn't think our new neighborhood would have so many kids," Tiana replied.

"I'm so glad it does. I love making new friends," said Briana.

4

The car finally stopped in front of a big house with a huge front yard.

"Well girls, we are finally here. I hope you like the new house!"

Both girls unhooked their seatbelts and bolted from the car's backseat. They knew right away which house was theirs because not only was it big and beautiful, but there were two bicycles in the front yard. The bikes were the girls' favorite colors. One was green and Briana knew that one was for her. The other was purple and it was obviously for Tiana. With smiles as big as the moon, the girls ran over to the bikes. Mrs. Taylor was glad to see both of her girls happy, even if it was only for a little while. She knew Tiana would find something to frown about, so she enjoyed the moment while it lasted.

Mom reminisced on the days when the girls were younger, the days when Tiana and Briana's unique attitudes and personalities were first identified by her and dad. By the time the girls turned two, Mr. and Mrs. Taylor not only knew their little girls shared the same beautiful chestnut eyes, warm brown cocoa skin, and luscious wavy hair, but also that the girls differed big time when it came to their attitudes. Briana was always a happy little girl who found joy in any and everything. Tiana, on the other hand, was feisty and found it hard to be happy most of the time. Mrs. Taylor, trying to find the positive in raising two girls, liked the fact that their very different personalities worked in their favor. Briana was more on the passive side and seemed to allow other children to push her around, but Tiana was there to stand up and defend her. While Tiana was quick tempered and quick to put others in their place, Briana was always there to calm Tiana down and reason with her. Mrs. Taylor loved that the girls balanced each other and she was glad that their differences made them unique and strong and formed an unbreakable bond between them.

"Girls how do you like the house?" mom asked as she turned to look at the girls. Paprika began barking and running around in a circle as if to say, "Don't forget about me. I love it!" Everyone laughed.

"I love it mom," Briana chimed in with the

barking.

"It's okay I guess," said Tiana.

"I am sure we'll all adjust and come to enjoy this new chapter in our lives. Let's go in and take a look around and maybe later you two can take your bikes out for a spin."

The Taylor family entered their new home and each had their own thoughts about the new journey they were about to experience.

Chapter 2:
"What's Her Problem?"

CHAPTER 2

Tiana and Briana ran outside after hearing a lot of commotion. Paprika and an unfamiliar bark could be heard along with a woman's voice. She was yelling, but Tiana and Briana weren't quite sure what she was yelling about. As they stood on the porch at the top of the steps, they noticed a small tan and white dog with a big black bow on top of her head. She barked as loudly as she could at Paprika while the black bow bounced about in every direction. Paprika barked back, but his bark wasn't nearly as loud as the other dogs bark. The dog with the big black bow was attached to a leash that was in the hand of a woman who wore all black as to match her dog. As Tiana and Briana descended the stairs, the strange woman turned to face them and she didn't look pleased at all.

"Is this your dog?"

She asked, looking from one girl to the other, all the while tapping her shoe on the concrete.

Both girls looked at one another before speaking. Their eye contact signaled to the other whose personality would be best for the situation. The lady dressed in black seemed a little grouchy, so Tiana decided it would be best for her to speak.

With a bit of sassiness in her voice, Tiana replied. "Yes, it is. Why?"

The lady dressed in black didn't say anything for a moment. She simply looked from Tiana to Briana with raised eyebrows and a frown.

"Well first, let me say my name is Ms. Perfect and I am your next door neighbor. This is Princess," she said pointing to her dog.

"I thought I heard voices over here and I knew the place had been bought, so I came over to introduce myself."

Ms. Perfect's tone then changed. "I didn't know there would be children and a dog."

Tiana sensed the woman had ill feelings about children and dogs, but couldn't understand the bad feelings about dogs since she owned one herself. Ready to match Ms. Perfect's attitude with her own,

Tiana was prepared to speak until Briana poked her in the back.

"It is nice to meet you Ms. Perfect and Princess. I'm Briana and this is my identical twin, Tiana. We are the only children living here with our parents and grandma."

It seemed as if Ms. Perfect's facial expression softened a little, but not much. "Well just to let you both know, this block of Sycamore has no children on it. Well, it hadn't had any children until you two and I was the only one on this block to have a dog," Ms. Perfect continued.

"Well it has both now, children and another dog," Tiana said in a matter-of-fact tone.

Briana looked at her sister and they both realized what Ms. Perfect's problem was. First, she didn't like children. Why? They didn't know. Secondly, she liked the fact that Princess was the only dog on the block, but now she had to share the block with Paprika. Before Tiana and Briana could say another word to Ms. Perfect, they heard the screen door open and out stepped their mother.

"Is everything alright out here?"

Mrs. Taylor waited for a response as she descended the steps. She looked at the girls and then at Ms. Perfect.

Ms. Perfect was the first to speak. "As I was just telling your children, I came over to introduce myself."

The girls decided to let their mother continue the conversation with Ms. Perfect and they began walking away.

"Excuse me girls. Where are your manners? Say goodbye to Ms. Perfect."

The girls turned and said goodbye, even though they didn't want to be around her for another minute and then they went into the house.

"I don't know what her problem is," Tiana said as they sat on the floor of their new bedroom because their furniture had not yet been delivered.

"I think she may not like kids all that much or maybe it's just that there has never been any children on this block before and she's not used to having kids around," Briana said calmly.

"Well, she'd better get used to it and fast. I didn't want to move here in the first place and I don't want to add this lady to my list of reasons why."

Tiana was getting mad and Briana didn't like when Tiana got mad.

"Calm down Tiana. Getting mad is not going to solve anything. Maybe what we should do is talk to Ms. Perfect and find out why she doesn't like children or at least hear her side of the story before we go letting our emotions get out of control."

Briana knew there had to be some kind of story behind Ms. Perfect not liking kids because people aren't born like that. She knew something must've happened in Ms. Perfect's life to make her feel this way and if she and Tiana could figure out why, they could change Ms. Perfect's way of thinking and change her feelings toward kids. There was just one problem. How would they find out because Ms. Perfect wasn't going to willingly tell them her story? She probably wasn't even going to let them get close enough to her to ask her a thing.

"So what should we do then?" Tiana asked as

if reading her twins mind.

"Maybe you're right and something did happen to her that made her dislike kids." Tiana stopped herself. "Hey! Why do I even care if Ms. Perfect likes kids or not? In fact, I don't care. She will just have to get used to the fact that we are here and we are here to stay."

Tiana turned to leave the empty room she and her sister shared.

"Wait Tiana, I care." Briana waved her hand as a signal for Tiana to come back and listen to what she had to say.

"Listen Tiana, I know you are upset about moving here, but we are here now and it seems that we will be here for a long time. I don't want to live next door to a lady who doesn't like me. It will make our lives miserable. We need to do something to make her understand that children aren't so bad."

Tiana rolled her eyes. Briana let out a sigh and continued speaking her thoughts aloud.

"Tiana just hear me out. Do you want to have this lady always watching our every move or always having something to say when we are outside trying to have fun?"

Not giving Tiana a chance to answer, Briana continued. "What about telling everything to mom and dad, huh?"

Briana could see that Tiana was beginning to understand what was being said. Tiana came further into the room and walked toward the window. While looking out, she could see Ms. Perfect outside still speaking with their mother. As if knowing Tiana was looking out the window, Ms. Perfect looked up in Tiana's direction. Tiana quickly moved away from the window not wanting to give Ms. Perfect any indication that they were talking about her.

"Besides Tiana, we were brought up to love our neighbor as we love ourselves. If Ms. Perfect is going through something, don't you think it's our duty to help her? Mom, dad, and grandma taught us that and they would expect it from us."

"Maybe Briana had a point. She was always the voice of reason and truth," Tiana thought to herself. Briana always knew what to say when Tiana was being difficult and hard headed.

Turning to face her sister, she agreed, "Okay. What did you have in mind?" Briana took a second to think about the question.

"Well, we could ask her over for coffee and maybe some of mom's delicious sweet potato pie."

With her hand on her hip, Tiana asked, "How do you know she likes coffee?"

"Because all grownups like coffee, that's why. Grownups love to see children acting like children and not being disrespectful. Maybe she's had a bad experience with children and now she thinks all children are the same. Once she sees how well behaved we are and how helpful we are with mom and grandma, she will soon agree that children can't be all bad. She may even loosen up a bit and tell us why she doesn't like children and we won't even have to ask her anything."

Tiana thought it was a ridiculous idea and began telling Briana that exact point. "You think it's gonna be that easy, huh? You think this lady will come over, eat pie, drink coffee and begin telling us her life story? Really Briana and they say you're the smart one. At this moment, I can't tell."

Feeling insulted, Briana replied, "Do you have a better idea? At least it's worth a try."

Tiana had to admit she didn't have any ideas at all. As if admitting defeat, Tiana shrugged her shoulders.

"Okay, so what do I have to do?" Briana smiled and began to tell Tiana of her plan. As Briana shared the details, Tiana had a bad feeling that things were not going to go quite as planned. She hated when she got those feelings because most of the time she was right. Just this once she hoped she was wrong.

CHAPTER 3

The girls decided the best time to have Ms. Perfect over for questioning was after dad arrived with the furniture. He would be arriving to the new house in a few days and he and mom would start setting up the furniture. So until the furniture arrived, the girls would keep an eye on Ms. Perfect. They would watch her every move to see if they could figure anything out from the information they gathered. It wasn't easy at first. Ms. Perfect was an early riser and did most of her errands long before the girls got up in the morning. The one thing she did faithfully every four hours was walk Princess. Tiana and Briana followed her a few times as she walked Princess in the same direction every time. This was a routine that Princess was all too familiar with because, at times, it appeared that Princess was walking Ms. Perfect instead of the other way around. To make things look normal and so that Ms. Perfect wouldn't think anything strange, Tiana and Briana took Paprika with them on their little investigation. That was the worst idea ever. As they trailed behind Ms. Perfect, all while keeping their distance, Paprika spotted Princess and immediately took off to be near her. Paprika pulled Briana so fast and so hard that he almost dragged her, all the while barking like he lost his mind. Of course all of this caught Ms. Perfect's and Princess' attention and Ms. Perfect was not at all happy about the commotion. She turned to the girls and her facial expression said it all. Meanwhile, Paprika was trying his best to get close to Princess, but she wasn't having it. Princess moved closer to Ms. Perfect while Briana tried to get Paprika under control.

"Could you please get control of your dog? He is making Princess upset."

Briana did the best she could, but Paprika was not cooperating at all. After a few moments of Paprika and Briana running around in circles and Ms. Perfect becoming angrier by the minute, Paprika calmed down and gave up the idea of getting close to Princess.

"This is why I've enjoyed a childfree and dog-free street," Ms. Perfect replied as she huffed and rushed passed the girls like she was late for an appointment.

"Wow! That went well," Tiana replied with all the sarcasm she could muster up.

"Any other bright ideas Briana? This one went so well I just can't wait to hear what else is next on your to do list."

Briana knew Tiana was mad, but it wasn't like she planned for things to go the way they did.

"Okay Tiana. That did not go as planned, but we can't give up. We'll have to keep trying," Brianna responded trying her best to be encouraging.

Next time she'd put more thought into this detective business and leave Paprika at home. Besides, they didn't learn anything on this outing that brought them any closer to knowing why Ms. Perfect didn't like kids. Briana pulled Paprika in the direction that Tiana was already headed, home.

CHAPTER 4

The girls decided to take a break from private detective work and tour the neighborhood. It was a much needed break because they only managed to upset Ms. Perfect and maybe give her more of a reason to not like children. They particularly wanted to see the park they spotted when they first got into town. The girls told their mom that they were going site seeing as they grabbed their bikes from the front porch. They never wanted to upset mom, at least Briana didn't. They always told her where they would be when they weren't in her presence. Tiana didn't like to upset mom either, but she needed a little more persuading to follow the rules. Tiana was more of a free spirit than Briana. She felt rules were made to be broken, as long as no one got hurt of course.

As the girls approached the park, they could hear the laughter and excitement of the children. The closer they got, the louder the laughter became and the girls were even more eager to get there. Once they arrived, Tiana and Briana found there to be lots of children playing. The girls dropped their bikes next to a park bench and a sign that read *Pine Valley Recreational Park*. They looked at each other and then surveyed the park as they tried to determine what area to visit first. The park had lavish, green grass which was freshly cut and a huge slide that shined as the sun bounced its ray off of it. It also had several swings that were all occupied at the time and a seesaw that was at their disposal if they wanted it. There were plenty of park benches for parents to sit and supervise their children while talking to other parents who were there doing the same things. There was a basketball court and a baseball field that could be used for soccer too. The park was beautiful and the girls knew it would be a place they would spend a lot of their time.

The girls decided to ride the seesaw first. As they approached it, two boys were thinking the same thing and both the girls and boys reached it at the same time.

"We got here first," Tiana said with a tone that

should have warned the boys to keep silent and to find something else to ride. The boys did neither.

"You were not here first because we were," replied one of the boys.

Both boys appeared to be about nine or ten which was about the same age as the girls. The girls were ten and had just celebrated their birthdays two months prior in April. They'd just completed the fourth grade and in the fall would start the fifth grade.

"We came to play on this seesaw and we are going to do just that. I suggest you turn around and get moving," Tiana said and again with major attitude.

Briana, being the person she was, didn't want any trouble and decided going back and forth with the boys wasn't worth the hassle.

"Tiana let's just check out the rest of the park and let the boys play on the seesaw and we can come back later," Briana said hoping Tiana would just move along without having to win this disagreement.

Somehow Briana knew that would probably

not be the case. Tiana just had to have the last word and win all the arguments. Briana, on the other hand, was easy going and she simply wanted to compromise so everyone would be happy. The two boys looked at Tiana to see if she would cave in and give up, but when she put her hands on her hips they knew no such thing was going to happen.

The boy who spoke earlier seemed to have an attitude to match Tiana's. He had blonde hair and green eyes and was just a little taller than the girls. The other boy who didn't say a word the entire time was Asian and seemed to not want any trouble. He had dark hair and dark, affectionate eyes. He appeared to be a little on the shy side.

"Let's just let the girls play on it Max and we can play on it later," said the Asian boy.

He seemed to be the voice of reason amongst the two, just like Briana was.

"We don't have to do anything Brandon. We were here first and we're not budging," Max said.

They all stood there looking at one another. Max and Tiana glared at one another, waiting to see who would back down first. Brandon and Briana wanted to leave them both standing there and come back later to see how it all worked out.

"I want to play some more before I have to go in and eat dinner," replied Brandon as he walked away.

Max didn't like the fact that Brandon always backed down and looked like a wimp in the process. He hated it even more that, by association, he looked like one as well. He felt like he had to always prove this otherwise and that was a pain most of the time, but they'd been friends since Kindergarten and no matter what their differences were they would always remain friends.

"Wait up Brandon," said Max sighing as he ran after him.

As the boys ran along, the girls climbed on each end of the seesaw and began riding. Briana didn't like that they were only at the park for five minutes and already they had made enemies. The dispute didn't seem to faze Tiana at all. She laughed and threw her head back as the seesaw went up and down. Afterwards, the girls walked around taking in the sights. They passed Brandon and Max a few times. Max gave the girls dirty looks while Brandon remained neutral. Briana didn't like that they lived next door to a lady who didn't like kids and now they had two neighborhood boys who didn't like them either. Just as the girls decided to head home, Brandon approached Briana.

"You're new to Pine Valley?" Brandon asked, almost apologetically.

"Yes we are. We moved from Philadelphia," replied Briana.

"I'm Brandon. What are your names?"

"I'm Briana and my twin's name is Tiana. I'm sorry about what happened earlier. My sister can be a handful at times. Actually, most of the time," Briana said laughing. Tiana didn't like her comment at all and the look she gave Briana told her such.

"I know what you mean. My friend Max is the same way." Tiana gave Brandon the same look she'd just given Briana.

"So, what grade are you in?" asked Brandon.

"We're going to the fifth grade and we're starting Pine Valley Elementary School in the fall," replied Briana.

"Max and I will be in the fifth grade too and we're attending Pine Valley Elementary School too," Brandon said with a little more excitement in his voice. Now it was Tiana's turn to chime in.

"Well isn't that just great. We're going to be at the same school and in the same grade as these two. What next, the same class?"

Tiana wouldn't let up and Briana had to put an end to it all and make her see she was being unreasonable.

"Okay, enough Tiana! Brandon did nothing to you and you need to stop giving him attitude right now."

Tiana knew by the tone of Briana's voice that she must have been out of control. Briana only stepped in when Tiana reached the point of needing a reality check. As Tiana began to speak, Max walked over to the group. He didn't even look at the girls, but he directed his attention and question to Brandon.

"Everything okay Brandon?"

"Everything is fine Max. I was just talking to Briana and Tiana. Guess what Max? The girls are going to be our classmates."

Max had a look that neither Tiana or Briana could figure out. Was it the look of shock or disinterest? They didn't know. What Max said next left them to wonder no more.

"Is that so? Well, I've never seen either of you around here before, so you must be new."

Max seemed to have calmed down and he sounded sincere in his words. Maybe Max wasn't so bad after all, thought Briana. On the other hand, Tiana was a little less trusting and she didn't trust Max at all. Briana spoke up first.

"Yes, we are new. We just moved here from Philadelphia."

Max raised an eyebrow.

"Why did you move here?" asked Max.

Tiana, not liking Max's question, thought he was implying that they shouldn't have moved here in the first place.

"We're here because our father's job moved us here. We don't like it any more than you do."

Not wanting another disagreement to start, Brandon and Briana both began to speak.

"I think we should be going," replied Briana.

Both Brandon and Briana looked at one another and smiled. No one said a word for a few moments and then Max surprised everyone.

"Listen guys! I know we got off to a bad start, but I'm really not that bad of a guy. I'll admit I do have a temper and sometimes I may not handle problems in the best way, but I'm working on it."

Tiana and Briana looked at one another with a look of amazement. Brandon didn't look shocked at all by what Max had just said.

Brandon and Max had been friends for a long time. He knew Max had anger issues, but despite that they remained the best of friends. Brandon was the one who managed to calm things when Max's temper escalated. Max waited for a response from one or both of the girls, but neither Tiana or Briana said a word. Max took that as a sign that they didn't want

31

anything to do with him, so he started to walk away.

"Wait," said Tiana. "I know exactly how you feel. I tend to have some issues with my attitude and it gets me into trouble often. At least I have a twin to intercept for me and it seems you have someone to do the same for you," Tiana stated while giving Brandon a look of acknowledgement.

Everyone laughed. This broke the ice for both the girls and the boys. They all ended up walking over to the picnic table and talking a little while longer as they learned some interesting things about each other. For instance, Tiana learned she was more like Max than she thought. He got into trouble with his parents and in school because of his smart mouth and attitude. Briana learned a little about Brandon as well. His favorite subject was math and he hated school lunch, so he brought his lunch from home. They all exchanged information about themselves and the group seemed to get along better, compared to their earlier interactions. With all the talking between the girls and the boys, the topic of Ms. Perfect came up and the girls shared how they thought she didn't like kids.

"Do either of you know anything about Ms. Perfect or her situation? We hadn't done anything to her and she didn't like us the moment she laid eyes on us," Briana said.

"I don't care much for her or her pesky dog either," Tiana added.

"We've seen Ms. Perfect and her dog Princess walking through the neighborhood and I know most of the kids around the neighborhood won't go near her because she's mean to them. Why she's so mean, I don't know," said Brandon.

"I have no clue either, but what I do know is I have been living in this neighborhood since I was born and she has always been like that. All the kids are glad they don't live on the block with her. As far as we know, there are no kids on her block," replied Max.

"Well, there are now and you're looking at two of them," Tiana said pointing to herself and Briana.

"Oh no!" said the boys at the same time.

"Oh yes," replied Briana.

"Wow! I feel bad for you guys. That's not cool, not cool at all." Brandon said shaking his head.

"I don't want to live in this neighborhood with a woman who will make my life miserable," said Briana.

Tiana added, "We need to find out what her problem is with kids so we can confront her with it."

Tiana and Briana told Max and Brandon of their plan to get to the bottom of the situation. They shared the story of the fiasco that happened earlier and how following her didn't get them any information.

They told the boys that maybe following her and seeing where she went and what she did might give them a clue as to what her life was like and help solve the problem. If that didn't work, they were preparing to invite her over and show her that kids really weren't all that bad and because they intended to do this by being on their best behavior and serving her coffee and their mom's sweet potato pie. Mom's sweet potato pie was like a truth serum. People took one bite and they seemed to spill their guts afterwards. The sat around for hours talking, not wanting to go home. The girls hoped Ms. Perfect would open up about her life so that their move to the new town would be a pleasant one. If that didn't work, they didn't know what they would do next. After hearing the girl's story, the boys thought maybe they could be of help.

"Maybe we could help," said Brandon.

Max looked at Brandon with a raised eyebrow.

"And how exactly can we help, Mr. Detective?" asked Max.

"That's exactly it Max. We can be detectives and gather clues without Ms. Perfect having any idea as to what we are up to. While the girls are entertaining her, we can ask around about her. Somebody has to know something. She has lived here longer than we have, so the people around here have to know something about her, right? The girls can't ask around because they don't know anyone yet and that would make things difficult."

Brandon became excited just thinking about it. He loved helping people and the idea of being a detective sounded thrilling. Everyone pondered on what Brandon said. He did make sense. The mystery of Ms. Perfect could be solved quicker if there were more people on the case.

Tiana was the first to speak up. "I think Brandon has the right idea. We didn't have any say in moving here, but we can have a say in how happy we're going to be now that we are here."

They all agreed and the four of them put their heads together and came up with a plan to get to the bottom of why Ms. Perfect didn't like kids and to show her how totally wrong she was.

Chapter 5:
"Mind Your Own Business"

CHAPTER 5

Dad had been home for approximately two days now and the girls were so glad to see him. Earlier he was in their old town tying up loose ends. Mom made a big meal to celebrate the family arriving safely to the new house and everyone finally being under the same roof at one time. Mom and grandma went all out by preparing roasted chicken, peas, homemade macaroni and cheese and biscuits. Mom also made peach cobbler for dessert. Dad was extremely happy to be home with the family instead of away on a business trip. He showed just how much he missed mom's cooking by eating two servings of everything, including dessert. After dinner, the family sat around talking and then praying before going to bed.

The girls were happy to be sleeping in their comfortable beds again now that dad had set up the furniture in their room. Before dad arrived with the furniture, they had all been sleeping on air mattresses. The girls plundered through boxes and arranged all of their things. They put their things in places they thought would make their room similar to how their room at the old house was. Mom and grandma emptied the boxes containing items for the living room, kitchen, and dining room. Dad took care of the outside and organized the garage with the equipment he'd use to keep the yard looking nice. He then placed tools in places he could easily get to just in case a repair was needed inside the house. Everyone was busy making the house a home. Briana made the beds and Tiana put their collection of butterflies on the windowsill.

The girls were glad their room was finally in order and now they could put the next part of their plan into action. They wanted their mom to invite Ms. Perfect over for coffee and pie and while she was there, they would demonstrate just how purposeful kids could be and maybe even ask a question or two. Hopefully, they'd get to the bottom of why she didn't like kids. Tiana knew her mother would become suspicious if she asked her to invite Ms. Perfect over. Rarely did Tiana express interest in the neighbors and mom would surely wonder why there was a sudden interest.

"I think it would be best if you asked mom to invite Ms. Perfect over," said Tiana.

Briana raised her head and looked at her twin.

As if reading her mind, Tiana said, "You know if I ask mom, she'll immediately become suspicious."

Briana thought about this for a minute and realized it was true. Tiana rarely wanted to do anything nice for anyone, unless of course she benefited somehow from it. Mom would probably ask lots of questions. The only questions the girls wanted to hear the answers to were those that would bring them closer to understanding Ms. Perfect a little better.

"Alright, I guess you're right. I'll ask mom," said Briana.

Tiana gave her a smile and placed a brightly colored butterfly on the windowsill.

Eventually mom asked Ms. Perfect over for coffee and pie, but she was highly suspicious about why we wanted to have a woman we just met over for a kindly chat. Mom mentioned we never seemed to care about getting to know our neighbors before and the girls knew she would say something along those lines. We told her we thought we got off to a bad start with Ms. Perfect and since we had to live next door to her, we thought it only right to make it up to her. After all, we weren't lying. Mom gave in, but not before giving the girls a few once over looks that signified she wasn't buying any of it. Ms. Perfect accepted the invite and now stood on the Taylor's front porch. The girls heard the doorbell and immediately ran downstairs. Mom was just opening the door as the girls reached the last step.

The girls were dressed in purple and green matching dresses with matching flats on their feet and colorful headbands in their hair. They looked very pretty if they did say so themselves. Mom asked Ms. Perfect to take a seat at the dining room table when the girls entered the room. Mom glanced at the girls and did a double take. She didn't say anything at the time, but she was surely going to ask the girls what was really going on. The girls being dressed the way they were was a dead giveaway that they were interested in more than just being nice to Ms. Perfect. Tiana and Briana had on one of their "Sunday best" dresses, the ones they wore specifically for church. They knew by the look mom gave them that there was a conversation to be had once Ms. Perfect was gone. The girls walked further into the room and greeted Ms. Perfect.

"Hello again Ms. Perfect," the girls said in unison.

"Hello umm, Tiana and Briana isn't it?"

She gave the girls a once over as she said hello. The girls could tell she was impressed with how they were dressed. They knew that grownups loved to see children clean and dressed appropriately. The girls thought they were doing great with making a good impression on Ms. Perfect. They stood by their mom and asked if there was anything they could get for Ms. Perfect. Mom again gave them a look that said to the girls that something didn't seem right.

"Are you girls feeling okay," mom asked with a giggle.

"Of course mom. We just want to be helpful," replied Tiana.

Mom gave Tiana a "don't play with me girl" look. Tiana cleared her throat and went and stood next to Ms. Perfect.

"Ms. Perfect have you lived here long?" asked Tiana.

Before Ms. Perfect could answer, Briana interrupted.

"Let's not bother Ms. Perfect with a bunch of questions right now Tiana. Besides, she just got here and maybe she would like a cup of coffee and a slice of mom's scrumptious sweet potato pie," Briana said with a little nervousness in her voice. Briana wanted the magic of mom's pie to begin working on Ms. Perfect before the question and answer session began.

The girls waited for mom to close her mouth and to stop staring at them before they excusing themselves and heading into the kitchen to get what they needed to make Ms. Perfect's visit comfortable for her and rewarding for them. While they were in the kitchen, mom entered and asked what was really going on and why they were being so helpful.

The girls acted like they didn't have a clue as to what she was talking about. Mom told the girls she knew better and if they were up to some mischief, she would not be happy at all. She gave them an opportunity to confess, but the girls acted surprised because mom doubted their intentions. Mom dropped the issue, but only for the moment. Mom told the girls to get the pie and the utensils and place them on the dining room table and she'd be right behind them with the coffee cart. As the three of them headed back into the dining room with the necessities of a nice afternoon, the girls noticed Ms. Perfect looking at the pictures of them and the rest of the family that were scattered about on the dining room walls. Ms. Perfect turned to face them as if she was startled.

"Do you have any children Ms. Perfect?" mom questioned as she stopped near the table with the coffee cart.

The girls stopped in their tracks. Things couldn't have gone any better if they had planned it this way. Sure they planned the little gathering, but they didn't plan on mom playing such a major role. They wanted to ask the same question mom had just asked, but they didn't want to sound rude.

Mom found the perfect opportunity and saved the girls some time. The girls placed everything on the table as they waited for Ms. Perfect to answer. She seemed to have been in deep thought over the question or perhaps she just didn't hear it. Mom must've thought the same thing and she was prepared to ask Ms. Perfect again. When she finally spoke up, the girls were very disappointed with her answer.

"I don't like discussing my personal business," Ms. Perfect said matter-of- factly.

She said it in such a manner that no one knew how to respond. Ms. Perfect's response even seemed to catch mom off guard.

"Why don't you like to talk about yourself? How is anyone going to get to know you better if you don't talk about yourself?" Tiana said with frustration and annoyance in her voice. She wanted to get to the bottom of this and not waste any more time.

"Tiana, mind your manners," mom said with annoyance in her voice. Mom was a little lost as well and she wondered what she could've said that upset Ms. Perfect so.

"I think I'll be going," Ms. Perfect responded as she gathered her purse and headed toward the door.

Mom apologized and tried to get her to stay, but Ms. Perfect wasn't hearing it. She walked out the door and mom turned toward us with anger in her eyes. The girls looked at each other and knew they were in trouble and no more closer to solving the mystery.

Chapter 6:
"The Truth Comes Out"

CHAPTER 6

Mom said a prayer for Ms. Perfect after she sat the girls down and reminded them that they were raised to have manners and that they needed to go next door and apologize to Ms. Perfect for being rude. She said she could tell that Ms. Perfect was hurting on the inside and sometimes people who were hurting express it in many different ways on the outside. The girls asked what could be hurting Ms. Perfect, but mom said she wasn't totally sure. She said she knew when others were in pain and it was clear to her that Ms. Perfect was definitely in pain.

"Why did you two really want Ms. Perfect over here?" mom asked curiously. "And I don't want any of that, 'we just want to get to know the lady next door' mess. Got it girls?"

Tiana and Briana could tell that mom was not playing and that they should tell her the truth. The girls told mom that Ms. Perfect didn't like kids and that they wanted to show her that kids weren't so bad. Mom told the girls that they had good intentions and she was glad they cared enough to want to help, but that they should leave Ms. Perfect alone. She said if Ms. Perfect wanted them to know anything, she would have shared it with them and that it was obvious she was not ready to share anything. Mom encouraged the girls to pray for Ms. Perfect and to hope, that through praying, Ms. Perfect would be guided in the right direction and find what she needed to begin the healing process. The girls agreed they would pray for Ms. Perfect and they hoped she would find peace with whatever was troubling her.

Once mom was satisfied with her talk and the way the girls handled the conversation, she allowed them to go and apologize. The girls weren't happy with their mom's request, but they headed next door anyway.

Once the girls apologized to Ms. Perfect, mom allowed them to go to the park. The girls were hoping they would see Max and Brandon. They wanted to see what, if any, news the boys may have uncovered. The girls told their mom they would stay out of Ms.

Perfect's business, but they knew she wouldn't mind it if in the end, their involvement helped her heal. Besides, this is what their mother wanted for Ms. Perfect anyway.

On their way to the park, the girls discussed their visit to Ms. Perfect's house. When they knocked on her door earlier, Ms. Perfect didn't seem at all happy to see them and the girls expected her reaction to be just so. Princess was right at Ms. Perfect's heels with a matching look of dislike. The girls noticed how much Princess acted like her owner. It was as if she didn't like kids either. Princess even wore a bow that matched Ms. Perfect's dress. Princess was like a child to Ms. Perfect and she sure treated the dog like a child. The girls considered the similarities and thought that maybe this could possibly be the reason Ms. Perfect was so mean toward kids. Maybe she was not able to have children due to a sickness or maybe she never found a husband to have a family with and she thought it too late because she was older. Any one of these reasons would've been understandable for why Ms. Perfect was the way she was.

"Can I help you girls? I'm very busy," said Ms. Perfect.

"We wanted to apologize for what happened on this afternoon. We meant no disrespect," Briana said. She knew the apology would be better coming from her rather than Tiana. Tiana wasn't good at all with apologies.

"There was no harm done. I was being a bit emotional. If you don't mind, I would like to forget it ever happened. Thank you for coming by."

With that being said, Ms. Perfect closed the door. The girls wished the exchange of words had gone better, but they had to admit that things were probably going to get worse before they got better. The girls left and headed to the park. Sure enough Max and Brandon were sitting at a park table talking. The girls approached them at the table and took a seat.

"Hey guys! Find out anything interesting?" asked Tiana.

"We did," replied Max.

"We found out Ms. Perfect has lived in her

house for nearly twenty years now and she moved there with her husband and daughter," Brandon said.

"What! Husband! Daughter! What are you talking about?" exclaimed Briana.

Both girls looked at one another with curiosity in their eyes as they waited for Max and Brandon to continue.

"Yes, she was married with a daughter and then there was a fire." Before Max continued, he swallowed hard as if the words hurt to say.

None of the reasons the girls came up with explained Ms. Perfect's behavior. The girls would've never guessed that the reason was as horrible as what the boys were sharing with them.

"Ms. Perfect's house caught on fire while she was out of town at a teacher's convention. You see, we found out Ms. Perfect was a teacher at Pine Valley Elementary during the time of the incident.," Max continued.

The girls were shocked.

"Killed? Oh my goodness," said Tiana.

Mom was right. Ms. Perfect was in pain. The

girls were right too. They knew there was a reason she had ill feelings toward kids, but now they understood. Ms. Perfect lost her child and her husband in a fire and that would be devastating to anyone. How could such a thing happen?

"How did you guys find this information out?" Tiana asked.

"We asked our parents what they knew of Ms. Perfect and they told us of the fire. Then we looked up the information about the fire online and found a story about it in the Pine Valley Times. Apparently, the Perfect's had just had some work done in the house the same week and the fire was caused by faulty wiring. The family had not had a chance to put the batteries back into the smoke detectors because of the work being done in the house and as a result, Mr. Perfect and Camille died in their sleep."

Max was weary after telling the story and the girls were just as weary from listening. Brandon pulled out a notebook and in it were some newspaper clippings. He slid them over to Tiana and Briana. The girls took a look at the clippings. One was a picture of the burnt house with a caption that read *Accidental Fire Takes Two Lives*. There was another clipping of what appeared to be photos of Mr. Perfect and Camille before their tragic deaths. The girl's mouths hung open in shock. The girls looked at the boys and then back at the picture of Camille. The little girl resembled them. She looked like she could have been an addition to their family, making them triplets. She looked to be about the same age as the girls were and she had facial features similar to theirs. Her nose, her eyes, and her hair, it was all too creepy for the girls. No one said a word. No one knew what to say. They all sat there trying to digest what they had just learned. Briana was the first to speak up.

"So what do we do now? How do we help Ms. Perfect?"

The girls realized that Ms. Perfect did in fact like kids, but she was in so much pain over her loss that she took it out on kids. Seeing the girls for the first time must have triggered some familiar, but unwanted feelings for Ms. Perfect. It must have been a shock for her to see Tiana and Briana, knowing they resembled her own daughter so much. Now they knew Ms. Perfect's story and a tragic one it was. The girls understood and they needed time to figure out what to do. They thanked Max and Brandon for all their help and quietly rode their bikes home.

Chapter 7:
"Girls To The Rescue"

CHAPTER 7

The girls went straight to their room after arriving home. Mom told them that dinner would be ready in an hour, but the girls were not the least bit hungry. Tiana and Briana lay there on their beds, each in their own thoughts staring at the ceiling, but both thinking the same thing. What were they going to do? They truly wanted to help Ms. Perfect deal with her pain, but they didn't know where to begin.

As the girls continued to lay there on their beds, mom yelled for them to come downstairs. They jumped up quickly and rushed down the stairs.

"What's going on mom," asked Tiana.

The girls entered the living room, but they didn't realize Ms. Perfect was sitting on the couch and appeared to be upset. Immediately, the girls thought they were in trouble. They looked at Ms. Perfect, then over at mom, dad, and then grandma. Whatever happened must've been really been bad because the looks on their faces said so.

"We didn't do anything mom, honestly," said Tiana.

"Hush little girl and go sit down. No one said you did anything."

Everyone waited for the girls to sit before dad spoke up.

"Girls, something terrible has happened to Ms. Perfect and we want to see if you can help in any way. Ms. Perfect's dog, Princess, is missing and she is very upset right now. She wanted to know if either of you saw her?"

Both girls hesitated and looked at Ms. Perfect before answering. They both felt horrible after having heard the news. Ms. Perfect didn't need any more grief in her life, especially after all that she'd been through. It was devastating enough to have lost her family, but now the only family she knew was missing. It appeared she had been crying because her eyes were red and swollen. Mom placed a tissue between her and Ms. Perfect.

"The last time we saw Princess was this afternoon when we visited Ms. Perfect. We haven't seen her since," replied Briana.

Briana looked at Ms. Perfect and then over at her parents after speaking. Ms. Perfect, as if reading the girls minds, told them that she had taken Princess out for a walk right after they left. When she finished walking Princess, she left her in the back yard for just a few minutes to get something to drink. When she returned, Princess was gone. She had no idea how Princess had gotten out or where she could've gone. Ms. Perfect explained that Princess would never have just run off. Since the girls didn't have any answers for Ms. Perfect, mom allowed them to go back to their room. Tiana and Briana told Ms. Perfect how sorry they were and excused themselves.

Once the girls got back to their room, they knew immediately what they had to do. They had to find Princess. Tiana sat at her desk and took out a notebook. She scribbled *Operation Rescue Princess* on the top. The girls put their heads together and came up with ideas on what to do. They knew they would also need Max and Brandon's help again and they were glad that they all exchanged numbers before leaving the park earlier. They intended on giving the boys a call later and informing them of the plans.

The girls needed to make this right for Ms. Perfect. She had been through enough already. The girls were being a little selfish as well. They thought that if they found Princess for Ms. Perfect, she would change her attitude toward them. Helping Ms. Perfect could also be the beginning of a relationship between her and the girls. Tiana and Briana realized they really wanted a relationship with this woman, a woman they barely knew. They knew she needed them more than she realized and they really wanted this opportunity to help her. The girls may not have been able to bring her family back or take the place of her daughter, but they could be more of a family than she had at the present. Maybe that was just what she needed, a family who cared and loved her. Maybe with Ms. Perfect's help, Tiana and Briana would grow into lovely ladies like her daughter, Camille, would've been. If the girls were able to bring Princess back to Ms. Perfect, it could possibly be a way to break the ice and soften her heart. It would be a road to healing for Ms. Perfect and they wanted to pave the way for her.

CHAPTER 8

The following day the girls immediately went to work with Max and Brandon. On last night they all agreed to meet at the park this afternoon. Tiana and Briana filled the boys in on situation with Ms. Perfect and Princess and what needed to be done. The girls were to put up flyers letting the neighborhood know Princess was missing and since they didn't have a picture of Princess, they would have to put Tiana's drawing skills to good use. The boys would do what they did best and question the people in the neighborhood and since they knew the neighborhood so well, they could keep an eye out for Princess during their travels.

Everyone agreed to meet back at the park before dinner to see if there were any new developments. The boys jumped on their bikes and headed off to gather information and the girls headed home to make flyers to post in the neighborhood. The girls realized that they may have to dip into their

63

allowance for the cost of copying the flyers. They were each saving for something special, but they knew this was more important than anything else at the moment. They headed home to begin making the best flyers with hopes that they would reunite a woman with her dog because they really needed each other.

Before dinner, the girls completed the flyers and posted them throughout the neighborhood and without getting lost. They enjoyed walking through the neighborhood, seeing the sights, and becoming familiar with their surroundings. The girls soon learned that the other streets had kids living on them, but their street didn't have any until they arrived. The girls thought this was odd. Could it be that Ms. Perfect's heart was being protected all these years and now it was time for her to face her problems and heal? Is that the reason they were sent to Pine Valley? The girls pondered on these thoughts as they approached their house. Max and Brandon soon came barreling down the street toward them. They were out of breath as they jumped off their bikes and approached the girls.

"What's up guys? Why so dramatic?" Tiana asked.

The girls waited patiently for the boys to catch their breath and speak. Waiting was not a strong point of Tiana's and her patience started to wear thin.

"Today Max! Anytime now Brandon!" replied Tiana.

Max spoke up first. "We have some news about Princess."

"Really?" asked Briana excitedly.

"What have you heard?" she continued.

Brandon spoke up. "We were asking questions around the neighborhood about Princess and Kelly over on Green Street and she said she heard Jordan and Christopher talking about a dog and how they were going to teach a lady a good lesson."

"We think they were talking about Princess and Ms. Perfect," replied Max.

"What do you mean you think? Didn't Kelly tell you for sure?" Tiana questioned angrily.

"She said they wouldn't tell her all the details

for fear she would tell on them," Max replied seeing Tiana's temper rising.

"Don't get mad at us because she didn't know all the details. At least we got that much. I thought you would have been a little more grateful," Max said with outrage.

"Everyone just calm down! Max is right. We didn't have anything to go on and now we have a name or two and possibly a location for Princess," Briana said.

Tiana had to admit that Briana was right. Max and Brandon did bring them information that could possibly lead to them bringing Princess home and Tiana acted ungrateful. She apologized to Max and asked if he had anything else to share. The boys reported that Kelly thought that Jordan and Christopher had the dog and were planning to give the dog back after a few days. She said they wanted to teach the lady who owned the dog a lesson for being so mean to kids. Apparently the lady had a talk with Jordan's parents about him being disrespectful to her and her dog and he blamed the lady for the two week punishment he was placed on. Everyone thought the lady they were referring to sounded like Ms. Perfect.

"It wasn't Ms. Perfect's fault that his parents placed him on punishment. He should learn to respect his elders," Briana replied calmly.

Both the girls and the boys put their heads together and decided they'd go straight to the dognapper's house tomorrow and confront them. They were going to bring Princess home. They would have gone that very moment, but it was close to dinner time and the girls had to be home before dark. Confronting strange boys may not have been one of the best ideas the girls had come up with, but it was all they had. The girls contemplated telling their parents, but they quickly dismissed the idea because they knew how their mom felt about them getting involved in Ms. Perfect's personal life. Mom would've asked if they had any proof that Princess was taken by the boys and she would've told them that they had no right to barge over to someone's house and make demands. Even if Princess was there, the authorities needed to be alerted instead of the girls taking matters into their own hands. No one wanted the authorities involved and they didn't want Princess to be away from Ms. Perfect for another minute either. They truly believed Princess was with the boys and they would have to keep this adventure a secret, despite their parent's disapproval if they found out. They all agreed to meet at the park the next day and Max and Brandon would take them to the house they thought Princess was being held hostage.

Chapter 9:
"A Dog Is More Than A Dog"

CHAPTER 9

The next day couldn't have come fast enough for the girls. Before going to bed on last night, the girls said a prayer for Ms. Perfect and Princess. They prayed that they would be able to bring Princess home to Ms. Perfect and that she would be happy again. The girls asked mom if they could go to the park after breakfast and she agreed as long as they stayed out of trouble. The girls met Max and Brandon and followed them on their bikes to Jordan's house. When they arrived, they dropped their bikes and Tiana and Briana knocked on the door while the boys waited on the curb. After a minute or two, the door opened and a lady stood in the doorway.

"Can I help you girls," she asked.

"Yes, we came to see Jordan. Is he available?" Briana asked.

"I haven't seen you girls around here before. Are you new to the neighborhood?"

The lady looked past the girls and noticed Max

and Brandon standing on the curb. After speaking to the boys, the lady asked the girls to wait a minute while she got Jordan. A few minutes later a tall, dark-haired boy stood in the doorway. He looked the girls over and gave them a quizzical look.

"I'm Jordan," the boy replied.

The girls asked Jordan if they could talk to him for a minute. He shrugged and stepped out onto the porch.

"I understand you have a dog that doesn't belong to you," Tiana continued, getting right to the point.

Jordan was surprised by Tiana's comment, but he didn't confirm or deny it.

"Look, we already know you have Ms. Perfect's dog. If you give the dog to us, we won't tell anyone what happened or where we got her from. She belongs to a nice lady who really misses her," Tiana replied forcefully.

"Nice! Ms. Perfect has never been nice," Jordan said further proving to the girls that he did have something against Ms. Perfect and could have stolen her dog.

"You don't know what this woman has been through to make her the way she is. You have no idea," Briana said.

Jordan gave the girls a shrug demonstrating how much he really didn't care.

"Why should I care about Ms. Perfect or her dog? She's always walking that mangy mutt around the neighborhood being mean to all us kids. She acts like we did something to her. She even got me into trouble a few weeks ago," Jordan exclaimed.

"Well you shouldn't have disrespected her," Tiana replied angrily.

Jordan dismissed Tiana's comment.

"I don't understand that lady. I accidently hit her dog when I was playing basketball. She said we needed to be more careful and that we could've hurt her dog. I told her it wasn't done on purpose and she needed to calm down," spewed Jordan.

"You had no right talking to her like that. She cares deeply for her dog. Princess is like family and she is very protective of her," Briana replied.

"Well like I said, I don't care about her or her dog," Jordan reassured the girls.

"Jordan can we have just a moment of your time to tell you a story? If you don't feel differently about Ms. Perfect after we share her story, we will walk away and leave you alone. If your feelings change, then we want you to tell us what you know about Princess so that we can return her. Do we have a deal?" Tiana asked as she waited for Jordan's response.

Jordan didn't say anything. He looked at the girls to see if they were serious. He looked over at Max and Brandon. He'd known them for years and the look on their faces told him that the girls were serious.

"Okay. I will listen, but I never said I had her dog," Jordan stated.

They all looked at Jordan suspiciously before the girls started the story. They each took turns telling Jordan of Ms. Perfect's tragedy and how taking Princess only added to her grief. They explained that by taking Princess, Ms. Perfect wouldn't change. In fact, she may become even meaner toward kids. Jordan listened to the girls and he concluded that what they shared made sense.

Jordan asked the girls to wait on the porch for a moment and he would be right back. The girls looked at Max and Brandon with expectation in their eyes, hoping that they got through to Jordan and that he would return Princess. When the girls turned back around to face the door, they were greeted by a familiar bark. Jordan held Princess in his hands and released her when Briana reached for her. Tiana and Briana thanked Jordan and told him their mouths would remain silent concerning where they found Princess. They all left and headed home with a gift in tow.

Chapter 10:
"The Gift of Healing"

CHAPTER 10

Tiana knocked on Ms. Perfect's door and waited for her to answer. She opened the door and Tiana asked to come in and speak with her. Ms. Perfect didn't put up a fuss. She stepped aside and allowed Tiana to pass. Once inside, Tiana waited for Ms. Perfect to show her the way since she'd never been in her house before. It was nicely furnished, very clean, and well organized. Somehow Tiana knew Ms. Perfect wouldn't have it any other way. Ms. Perfect pointed to a chair and Tiana quickly took a seat.

"What brings you here?" Ms. Perfect asked.

"I wanted to apologize again for being so rude a few days ago. I'd planned on telling you that the first day we met, but Briana and I didn't think you liked us. Ms. Perfect I know about your husband and daughter and I am sorry for your loss. Now I know you don't dislike kids. It's just that you haven't gotten over your pain and like my mom says, 'hurt people hurt people'. I didn't quite understand what she meant then, but now I do."

Ms. Perfect didn't say a word, but her eyes filled with tears and Tiana continued.

"I wanted you to know that Briana and I can't bring your family back, but we can be like family to you. I know having lost Princess hasn't helped matters much either, so I have a surprise for you." Tiana stood and headed to the door to let Briana in. Ms. Perfect heard a sweet and familiar bark and she immediately ran to the door to meet Briana. Briana placed Princess in her arms and both girls watched as Ms. Perfect loved on Princess and Princess returned the same love to Ms. Perfect. After reuniting Ms. Perfect with her dog, Tiana and Briana headed home.

The following evening there was a knock at the Taylor's door. The family was preparing for dinner. Mom hated when people interrupted dinner. She stood to answer the door, but dad told her to relax and he'd answer it. Dad came back moments later and to all of their surprise, he had Ms. Perfect with him. He offered her a seat and she took it. She looked nervous, but there was something different about her.

The girls couldn't quite put their finger on it, but they knew this was a new Ms. Perfect, a Ms. Perfect who was on her way to healing.

Ms. Perfect started by saying how grateful she was that the girls found Princess and brought her home. She also shared how she had been living in pain with the loss of her family. She apologized for giving the girls the impression that she didn't like them and assured them that it didn't have anything to do with them. They looked so much like her daughter Camille and that took her by surprise. She wanted to be a good neighbor and she wanted a chance to start over. The Taylor family was silent after she was done speaking.

Ms. Perfect must have taken their silence as her cue to leave and she stood to do so. The girls rushed toward Ms. Perfect and stood next to her with big smiles on their faces. Mom and dad gestured for her to take her seat again, which she did.

"Let us help you begin your journey to healing by praying for you Ms. Perfect," mom urged.

The family held hands and prayed like they

had never prayed before. They prayed for healing for their new neighbor. They prayed that God would mend her broken heart caused by the of the loss of her family. They prayed for Ms. Perfect to begin enjoying life again and for her to experience happiness the way God intended and the way her family would've wanted it. They also prayed that this new relationship would blossom and grow into a family. When they were done praying, Ms. Perfect smiled and hugged mom and thanked her. She then looked at the girls and opened her arms wide. The girls ran to her and gave her the biggest hug and she welcomed it graciously. Everyone was silent for a moment, basking in the spirit. It was soon interrupted.

"Well, you are just in time for some of my daughter's delicious sweet potato pie," added grandma.

The girls giggled and soon everyone was laughing. This was one of Ms. Perfect's many dinners with the family. Dinner with the Taylor family helped to open the door for Ms. Perfect to begin the healing she desperately needed. Tiana and Briana were there to help when she needed a little shove in order to keep going. The girls, with the assistance of Max and Brandon of course, were proud to have solved the problem with Ms. Perfect.

Discussion Questions

1. Chapter 1- Although Tiana and Briana look exactly alike, their personalities are different. Using evidence from the text, describe how they are different.

2. Chapter 2- Ms. Perfect seems to have an attitude. What evidence from the text proves this? Predict why she has an attitude.

3. Chapter 3- The girls decide to play detective. What were they trying to find out? What evidence tells you this?

4. Chapter 4- Tiana and Briana meet Max and Brandon for the first time. What are some common traits that Tiana and Max and Briana and Brandon share? What text evidence tells you this?

5. Chapter 5- The girls invite Ms. Perfect over for coffee and pie. Why? State evidence from the text.

6. Chapter 5- Why does Ms. Perfect get so upset when Mrs. Taylor asked her about children? What evidence from the text tells you Ms. Perfect was upset?

7. Chapter 6- The truth comes out about Ms. Perfect. What is the truth? Find the passage that indicates this. How did the truth make you feel?

8. Chapter 7- Princess goes missing. What do the girls do to help find her? Give text evidence to support this.

9. Chapter 7- Why did the author have Princess go missing at this point in the story? How will finding Princess help Ms. Perfect?

10. Chapter 8- The girls find out Princess was kidnapped. Why was Princess kidnapped? Use text evidence to support your answer.

11. Chapter 8- The girls want to take matters into their own hands despite the opinion of their parents. Is this right or wrong? What would you do?

12. Chapter 9- Jordan doesn't admit to having Princess, but what evidence tells you he might have her?

13. Chapter 10- What changes do you see with Ms. Perfect from the beginning of the story till the end of the story? Use evidence from the text to support your response.

Author's Bio

Doreen Allen has always loved children. The idea of becoming a teacher was with her since she could think for herself. The aspiration of becoming a writer came about much later in life and Doreen managed to avoid it, at least until God placed it heavily in her spirit in 2015. By that time, Doreen had gone through many tough times in life. One of the darkest moments in her life was in 2005 when her daughter, Tiana, passed away. Doreen wanted a way to keep Tiana's spirit alive and in 2009 the inspiration came, but did not manifest until 2015. Doreen's love for God, children, and writing all manifested in the tale of Tiana and Briana: The Problem with Ms. Perfect. It is the first in her series of books dedicated to the spirit of her daughter Tiana.

Made in the USA
Middletown, DE
03 September 2019